W9-AUD-482

Simon & Schuster Books for Young Readers

PRESENTS

The Spider and the Fly

SIMON & SCHUSTER BOOKS FOR YOUNG READERS

New York   London   Toronto   Sydney   New Delhi

Based on the poem by **Mary Howitt**

With illustrations by **Tony DiTerlizzi**

"Will you walk into my parlor?" said the Spider to the Fly,

"'Tis the prettiest little parlor that ever you did spy;

The way into my parlor is up a winding stair,

And I have many curious things to show you when you are there."

"Oh no, no," said the little Fly, "to ask me is in vain,

For who goes up your winding stair can ne'er come down again."

"I'm sure you must be weary, dear, with soaring up so high;

Will you rest upon my little bed?" said the Spider to the Fly.

"There are pretty curtains drawn around; the sheets are fine and thin,

And if you like to rest awhile, I'll snugly tuck you in!"

"Oh no, no," said the little Fly, "for I've often heard it said,

They never, never wake again, who sleep upon your bed!"

Said the cunning Spider to the Fly, "Dear friend, what can I do,

To prove the warm affection I've always felt for you?

I have within my pantry, good store of all that's nice;

I'm sure you're very welcome—will you please to take a slice?"

"Oh no, no," said the little Fly, "kind sir, that cannot be,

I've heard what's in your pantry, and I do not wish to see!"

"Sweet creature!" said the Spider, "you're witty and you're wise,

How handsome are your gauzy wings, how brilliant are your eyes!

I have a little looking-glass upon my parlor shelf,

If you'd step in one moment, dear, you shall behold yourself."

"I thank you, gentle sir," she said, "for what you're pleased to say,

And bidding you good morning now, I'll call another day."

The Spider turned him round about, and went into his den,

For well he knew the silly Fly would soon come back again:

So he wove a subtle web in a little corner sly,

And set his table ready, to dine upon the Fly.

Then he came out to his door again, and merrily did sing,

"Come hither, hither, pretty Fly, with the pearl and silver wing;

Your robes are green and purple—there's a crest upon your head;

Your eyes are like the diamond bright, but mine are dull as lead!"

Alas, alas! how very soon this silly little Fly,

Hearing his wily, flattering words, came slowly flitting by;

With buzzing wings she hung aloft, then near and nearer drew,

Thinking only of her brilliant eyes, and green and purple hue—

Thinking only of her crested head—poor, foolish thing! At last,

Up jumped the cunning Spider,

and fiercely held her fast.

He dragged her up his winding stair,
into his dismal den,

Within his little parlor—
but she ne'er came out again!

And now, dear little children, who may this story read,

To idle, silly, flattering words I pray you ne'er give heed;

Unto an evil counselor,
close heart and ear and eye,

And take a lesson from this tale,
of the Spider and the Fly.

R.I.P.

Dear Sweet Creatures,

No doubt you've finished our delicious tale and are surprised by this little tragedy, but then again, what did you expect from a story about a spider and a fly? Happily ever after? Spiders are trappers, for goodness' sake! We've been doing it for generations, and we're quite good at it. Even your beloved Charlotte in E.B. White's classic Charlotte's Web admitted as much. But alas, the poor dear never capitalized on her fortune. Now if I were in her shoes, I would be eating bacon.

With the wealth of knowledge about spiders and our crafty, carnivorous ways, you'd think my web would be empty, but not a day passes without a hapless bug or two stopping by. What's a spider to do? To be completely fair, my most recent dinner guest put up a commendable fight. But I am a talented and persistent hunter with many schemes up my sleeves. And you can see, I always get my bug.

So what does all this talk of spiders and traps have to do with you? Be warned, little dears, and know that spiders are not the only hunters and bugs are not the only victims. Take what has transpired within these pages to heart, or you might well find yourself trapped in some schemer's web.

Bon appétit,

Spider

Mary Howitt

was born in Gloucestershire, England, in 1799. The daughter of devoted Quakers, Samuel and Ann Botham, she married William Howitt in 1821. Between the two of them, the couple authored more than 180 books. Of the two Howitts, Mary is generally considered to be the more accomplished, and Dickens himself invited her to contribute to his journal, *Household Words*. Mary's own books include *Sketches of Natural History, Ballads and Other Poems*, and several translations of the work of Hans Christian Andersen, including his fairy tales. During her distinguished career, Mary was associated with such renowned literary figures as Dickens, Tennyson, Wordsworth, and Browning. In addition, she and William are noted for helping poet John Keats get his start. In 1870, the Howitts retired to Italy where William died in 1879 and Mary in 1888.

The Spider and the Fly: An Apologue: A New Version of an Old Story first appeared in *The New Year's Gift* in 1829 and five years later in Mary Howitt's *Sketches of Natural History*. In the generations since its original publication, many have come to value this poem as a cautionary tale, and William Bennett, in his introduction to "The Spider and the Fly" in *The Moral Compass* (a companion to *The Book of Virtues*), says, "Unfortunately, as long as there's dishonesty in the world, there will be people ready to lay traps for us. We must learn to recognize them and guard against their wiles. Not everyone who talks sweetly offers sweets."

Tony DiTerlizzi,

bestselling author and award-winning illustrator, has been creating books with Simon & Schuster Books for Young Readers for more than a decade. From his fanciful picture books like *Jimmy Zangwow's Out-of-This-World Moon-Pie Adventure* and *G Is for One Gzonk!* to chapter books like *Kenny & the Dragon* and *The Search for WondLa*, Tony imbues his stories with a rich imagination. His middle-grade series The Spiderwick Chronicles, written with Holly Black, has sold millions of copies, has been adapted into a feature film by Paramount Pictures, and has been translated and distributed in more than thirty countries. For his decidedly Victorian take on Howitt's poem, Tony found inspiration in classic Hollywood film noir as well as the illustrations of Ed Gorey, Chaz Addams, and Tim Burton.

The illustrations that appear in this book were rendered using Lamp Black and Titanium White Holbein Acryla Gouache and Berol Prismacolor Pencil on Strathmore 5-Ply, Plate Bristol board and reproduced in silver and black duotone. The "ghosts" were created in graphite and then added as a transparent layer using Adobe Photoshop. Much thanks to designer Greg Stadnyk for putting it all together.

For Holly and Theodor Black, the quintessential gothic couple —T. D.

Tony would also like to thank: Kevin Lewis—this book wouldn't be here if it were not for your vision and faith in me—thank you: Stacy Leigh, Jennifer Lavonier, and Jon Scieszka, for all of your wonderful feedback and support; and my best friend/wife/boss/agent/critic/#1 fan, Angela.

SIMON & SCHUSTER BOOKS FOR YOUNG READERS · An imprint of Simon & Schuster Children's Publishing Division · 1230 Avenue of the Americas, New York, New York 10020
Illustrations copyright © 2002, 2012 by Tony DiTerlizzi · All rights reserved, including the right of reproduction in whole or in part in any form.
SIMON & SCHUSTER BOOKS FOR YOUNG READERS is a trademark of Simon & Schuster, Inc.
For information about special discounts for bulk purchases, please contact Simon & Schuster Special Sales at 1-866-506-1949 or business@simonandschuster.com.
The Simon & Schuster Speakers Bureau can bring authors to your live event. For more information or to book an event, contact the Simon & Schuster Speakers Bureau at 1-866-248-3049 or visit our website at www.simonspeakers.com.
Book design by Tony DiTerlizzi and Greg Stadnyk · The text for this book is set in Caslon Antique.
Manufactured in China · 0612 SCP · 10 9 8 7 6 5 4 3 2 1
CIP data for this book is available from the Library of Congress. · ISBN 978-0-689-85289-3 (original hc) · ISBN 978-1-4424-5454-5 (10th anniversary hc)

The End